WOODLAND

SHYLA'S
WOOD WIDE
WEB

EXPLORERS CLUB

Head of Zeus Ltd
First Floor East
5–8 Hardwick Street
London EC1R 4RG

WWW.HEADOFZEUS.COM

GF: *For Thea.*

EJ: *For Magda and Julia.*

**Also by Ewa Jozefkowicz**

*Woodland Explorers Club: Benji's Emerald King*

WOODLAND

SHYLA'S
WOOD WIDE
WEB

EXPLORERS CLUB

Ewa Jozefkowicz
illustrated by Gillian Flint

ZEPHYR

# THE WOODLAND EXPLORERS CLUB RULES

1) Our mission - to find out the secret power of mushrooms

2) Speak to each other using our secret owl hoot

3) Look out for each other

4) Respect and protect the forest and its animals

5) Discover what Willow Wish Woods was like hundreds of years ago! (Maybe we'll discover dinosaur bones!)

# CHAPTER 1
## A MAGICAL PRESENT

Shyla opened her eyes. A beam of sunlight streamed through the window after almost a week of rain. Just in time for her birthday!

She was sitting in her shed where she loved to paint. It was her special place – at the end of the garden, right next to Willow Wish Woods. From here she could see how the forest had changed. It had a magical way of doing that in the autumn.

## SHYLA'S NOTEBOOK

Autumn colours in Willow Wish Woods:

- Fiery red
- Vibrant orange
- Golden yellow
- Rusty brown
- Warm cinnamon
- Mellow mustard
- Pumpkin orange
- Chestnut brown
- Amber
- Olive green
- Mahogany
- Copper
- Harvest gold
- Tawny

Shyla was itching to draw the beech tree on the edge of the forest. Its leaves had turned from a warm yellow to a deep copper. She was taking out her favourite colouring pencils when her mum opened the shed door.

'Happy birthday!' she cried. She was carrying a tray filled with tasty treats. Raisin pancakes, crunchy pears cut into half-moons, just how Shyla liked them, and hot chocolate with marshmallows (Shyla's favourite lemon-flavoured ones). Her mum ran a bakery in town and there was always something yummy in the kitchen.

She handed Shyla her present. It was big, square, and rattled promisingly. Shyla held it to her ear, hoping it was what she thought it was – a set of coloured inks from the art shop in town. There was a brilliant shade of electric blue. It would be perfect for painting the kingfisher she had once seen near the Tadpole Run.

Shyla unwrapped the box and there it was! Colours shimmered at her – glowing gold, emerald green, ruby red.

'You're the most awesome mum in the world!' said Shyla, throwing her arms around her. 'I'll save them for my best pictures.'

'Don't do that.' Mum smiled. 'Use them every day to bring the birds to life!'

That was exactly what the Woodland Explorers tried to do – restore life to the beautiful forest on their doorstep. Shyla, her cousin Ajay, and her friends, Benji, Eric, Trix and Fujiko, had formed the club after hearing the music of an ancient oak hidden in the woods. They named the tree the Emerald King, and he'd helped them rescue a stag who was in danger. But they knew Braveheart, the stag, was only the beginning. Many animals had left the forest, and it was up to the Woodland Explorers to bring them back.

At 8.31 a.m. exactly, the doorbell rang and Shyla ran inside to open it. Ajay and his mum,

Shyla's Aunty Kali, picked her up for school every day with Benji and Eric. They'd worked everything out so nobody was ever late. Today they were a whole six minutes early because it was Shyla's special day.

'Happy birthday!' the three friends yelled, and Ajay did a funny robot dance.

'We have a present for you from the Woodland Explorers,' said Benji. 'But you'll have to wait until we're together at breaktime to open it.'

'Ooooh, but I *can't* wait,' said Shyla.

'You'll have to,' said Eric, laughing.

'I have something for you, too,' said Aunty Kali. 'We discovered this in your grandmother's bedroom. She would have wanted you to have it.'

'Wow, something from Nani?' Shyla had loved her grandma's house. It was full of treasures – from her childhood in India and her time spent in South America. She had died three years ago, and Shyla still missed her.

Shyla grasped the small package wrapped in silver paper.

'Shall I open it now?' she asked.

'Go for it,' said Mum.

Shyla sat on the stairs and felt the parcel. It was surprisingly heavy. She wondered if it was one of Nani's carved statues from Brazil? Or maybe the little vase with painted mermaids she had brought back from Australia? But when the last bit of sticky tape came undone, she saw it was a pair of black binoculars.

'Do you remember when Nani used them to watch birds from her bedroom window?' asked Ajay.

Shyla used to sit on the windowsill next to Nani who would whisper the names of the birds and point them out to Shyla. It felt so precious to hold the binoculars now.

'You'll see the birds more clearly when you're drawing,' said Aunty Kali.

'Take them to school!' said Ajay. 'Let's see what we can spot in the woods.'

Shyla ran to get a scarf so the binoculars wouldn't get damaged in her bag, and the gang set off.

In the playground, they met Fujiko and Trix who were excited to give Shyla their present. Fujiko had wrapped it carefully and carried it all the way to school so the paper wouldn't tear.

'We worked on it with my sister,' she said proudly. Fujiko's older sister wanted to be an artist, just like Shyla. But instead of painting, she loved making sculptures from different materials.

'Rip it open!' shouted Ajay. Shyla tore the tissue paper and found a wooden picture frame carved with the Woodland Explorers' initials.

Shyla gasped. 'It's beautiful!'

'What will you put in it?' asked Fujiko.

'My painting of the kingfisher. One of these

days I'll see him again.'

'You could look kingfishers up on your tablet,' suggested Eric. 'There'll be loads of photos.'

'It's not the same as watching them in real life,' Shyla explained. 'You have to see how they move and how their bodies catch the light.'

Pine Class gathered in Swallow Clearing as usual. The day was cold and crisp. The air smelled of fallen leaves, and Shyla craned her neck to search for birds that hadn't yet migrated.

There were still a few swallows and house martins, and Shyla's second favourite bird – the chiffchaff. They were tiny, but some flew all the way to Tunisia, Libya and Algeria in North Africa for the winter!

Shyla hoped Mr Mattison might tell them more about birds, but that day Pine Class were learning about mushrooms. Shyla didn't think mushrooms were that interesting. The only ones she'd seen in Willow Wish Woods were orange and grew on the sides of trees, which she found yucky.

But then Mr Mattison told them something that made her ears prick up. He introduced them all to the Wood Wide Web.

## SUPER WOODLAND FACT:

### The Wood Wide Web

Deep in the forest, hidden beneath the soil, lies a network called the Wood Wide Web. It is a complex web of communication and friendship. And guess who the secret messengers are? Mushrooms!

These fungi play an important role in connecting the trees and plants together, through tiny threads called hyphae. They create a vast underground network that allows the trees to share nutrients, water, and even send warning signals to one another.

'How cool is that?' asked Ajay. 'I had no idea trees could communicate!'

'They're incredible,' said Eric. 'Hey, my dad told me a great mushroom fact. Do you want to hear it?'

'Go on,' said Shyla.

'The largest living thing on earth is a mushroom! It's called a honey mushroom.'

'Seriously?'

'A humongous fungus!' said Ajay.

## SUPER WOODLAND FACT:

**The Biggest Mushroom in the World!**
In Oregon, America, there's a huge mushroom called
the Honey Mushroom. It spreads out over an area
that's as big as 480 football pitches. This fungus
has been growing for thousands of years!

## SUPER WOODLAND FACT:

**Can you spot these woodland mushrooms?**
But be careful not to pick them,
because some might be **poisonous!**

**Chanterelle:** the chanterelle mushroom is like a burst of
sunshine! Its cap is smooth and bright orange, like a funnel.
This mushroom is a favourite of deer and rabbits.

**Woodland Agaricus** (pronounced A-gar-i-cus): the woodland agaricus has a brown cap with white scales, like a cosy hat. It grows in the leaf litter and rich soil shaded by trees. Squirrels and mice find it delicious.

**Oyster:** the oyster mushroom has a fan-shaped cap, with shades of white, cream, or beige. This mushroom is a treat for insects like ants and beetles, contributing to the natural recycling process in the woods.

Mr Mattison led the class further into the forest to search for three different kinds of mushrooms. Even Shyla was a tiny bit curious. She'd never paid attention to them before!

'Let's all take a closer look,' said Mr Mattison, 'but be careful not to pick them. Some mushrooms are poisonous and could make us sick if we ate them. Now, I'd like you to each choose one of the three mushroom types and draw it in your notepad. Mark up anything interesting that you see.'

Shyla chose the chanterelles. They reminded her of sunflowers that were about to open. Their wavy edges were like the ruffles of a tiny skirt. Her fingers itched to draw them properly – not just for their class exercise, but for one of her own pictures. She fumbled in her pocket for a sketching pencil and found the binoculars. What a perfect moment to test them!

That's when she noticed the words around the eye piece:

*A good pair of binoculars is like a passport to another world.*

Did Nani come up with this?

Shyla gazed at the cluster of chanterelles through the binoculars, which now looked like giant trumpets. She noticed every groove and delicate curve.

And then, her heart skipped a beat. There was a spark among the golden caps, a tiny flutter.

'What are you looking at?' asked Eric.

'I'm not sure,' Shyla whispered, her heart thudding. 'But I think I might have seen a fairy.'

# CHAPTER 2
## THE PIXIE RING

Shyla didn't dare breathe. Maybe the sparkle was a glint of sunlight?

Eric gently took the binoculars from her hands and peered through them.

'I can't see anything... Maybe only you can?'

Shyla looked down at her binoculars. Had they really shown her something secret?

Later, as they sat around the Learning Tree in Swallow Clearing, Shyla tried to explain to the Woodland Explorers what she'd seen. The whole thing sounded so magical, she couldn't believe her own words.

'It was a sparkle, bright blue like the stone in my mum's ring. I saw two other glowing lights, but not as bright as the blue one.'

'Could it have been a message?' asked Benji.

'We need to go back to the mushrooms as soon as possible!' Trix shouted, forgetting where she was. A couple of children turned around to stare.

'Shh, Trix!' whispered Benji, putting a finger to his lips. 'We could come with you after school?' he said to Shyla.

'Great plan!' said Shyla.

But when school ended, Shyla's mum and Aunty Kali said they all had to go straight to the Whispering Lake because they had a surprise waiting for Shyla.

There was a picnic area next to the lake, and they'd brought Shyla's favourite food – cheese and crisp sandwiches, rainbow picnic pie and mini milkshakes. Fujiko played the guitar and they sang songs. Ajay even convinced Shyla to join him in his robot dance. It was the best party ever! Though Shyla's thoughts kept turning to the strange sparkling mushrooms. And now she couldn't get to sleep.

She went to the window to check if Ajay was awake. His house was two doors down from hers, and she could easily see his bedroom window.

But she couldn't see any light from his bedside lamp. Their back gardens were filled with inky darkness. All was still, apart from the occasional hooting of an owl.

Shyla opened her window and leaned out. Once, she had been lucky enough to see an owl close up. She'd almost screamed because it seemed as if the bird was staring right at her.

## SUPER WOODLAND FACT:

**Owls** have a superpower called night vision. Their eyes gather as much light as possible which helps them see clearly on the darkest of nights.

Owls can also rotate their heads 270 degrees, looking left, right, up, down, and even backwards, without moving their bodies!

Shyla peered into the trees beside her shed where she'd last seen the owl. Just then, she noticed a circle of lights. She blinked, but they were still there.

Taking the binoculars from her bedside table, she lifted them to her eyes.

At first, she thought the glowing shapes might be tiny cones. But as she zoomed in closer, she saw their shapes were uneven and their heads were balanced on stems. They were mushrooms! Though unlike any she had ever seen.

Suddenly, she spotted movement – a flutter of wings. There were other shapes, shimmering between the mushrooms. Were they glowing butterflies? She turned the dial on the binoculars, but she still couldn't make out what they were.

Shyla felt certain this was a sign. Could they *really* be fairies? Were they trying to tell her something? Could they somehow be connected to the Emerald King, the ancient oak? She had to find out more.

'Wow,' said Eric, as they met Fujiko at the school gates next morning. Shyla had told them everything. 'I think you might have seen a pixie ring.'

'A what?'

'A pixie ring. It's called a fairy ring too. There was one in a book of myths and legends my dad read to me! Some people say that pixie rings are a portal to another world!'

## SUPER WOODLAND FACT:

**Pixie rings**, also known as fairy rings, are circles of mushrooms that can be found in meadows and woodlands. Legend has it they are where fairies and pixies gather to dance and play. They are caused by fungus growing underground. Tiny threads called hyphae sprout and grow in the shape of a circle, appearing above ground as mushrooms! They can be small at first and get bigger as they grow older.

'No way!' Shyla thought of the words carved around the lens of her binoculars. *A good pair of binoculars is like a passport to another world.* Was Nani somehow helping her to find magic?

'We need to investigate now,' said Benji. 'This is the Woodland Explorers' next mission!'

'But the pixie ring was over at Bluebell Clearing. That's on the other side of the woods,' said Fujiko.

'We can sneak away to look at it,' said Eric. 'We're making a harvest collage today, so we can collect leaves for that along the way.'

'But we can't go that far on our own,' said Shyla. 'We're meant to stay near the Learning Tree.' She was desperate to see the pixie ring, but what if she had imagined it all?

'Yes, Mr Mattison will tell us off',' said Fujiko, drumming her fingers on her lunchbox.

Shyla knew this was a sign Fujiko was nervous. 'Don't worry, we won't get into trouble,' she said, squeezing her hand.

'And we'll be super quick,' said Ajay. 'I know the best route.'

'Let's see if every group can come back with at least seven different types of leaves!' Mr Mattison called, clapping his hands together. 'We can figure out which trees they came from before we get our hands dirty with some painting!'

As soon as Pine Class set off on their task, Ajay led the Woodland Explorers through the pine trees and across the bridge to Bluebell Clearing.

Just as they thought they'd gone unnnoticed, they heard a familiar voice. It was Leon. Shyla's heart sank. Leon was always trying to get them into trouble.

'Hey, where are you off to?' he asked, folding his arms.

'Mr Mattison said we couldn't leave Swallow Clearing,' added Cora, who followed Leon everywhere. A smirk appeared on her lips. Shyla knew Cora wanted to report them.

'Shhh...' Trix hissed, hands on her hips. 'I've found something interesting that we want to tell the class about later. We'll be back soon.'

'I don't think this is a good idea,' said Leon, sounding like Mrs Jay, their headteacher. 'We're worried one of you might get hurt, so we're going to tell Mr Mattison. We don't want to, but we *have* to.'

Shyla hated the thought of being told off and wanted to turn back. But it was as if an invisible thread was pulling her towards the fairy ring. It was more important than anything else.

'Fine, go and tell him,' she said. Leon's eyebrows shot up in surprise.

'Run!' shouted Ajay, and the Woodland Explorers rushed forward, hoping Leon and Cora wouldn't catch them. They ran as fast as they could until Bluebell Clearing was in sight.

Soon the footsteps behind them stopped, and Shyla breathed a sigh of relief.

'Where did you see the mushrooms?' asked Eric.

'Just here,' she said, running into the clearing. 'To the left of the old willow tree.'

She looked around, panicking. What if they had disappeared?

'Woah. Over here,' said Fujiko. And there it was.

A perfect circle. Although on a cloudy autumn day, they didn't look half as magical to Shyla as they had the night before.

'When I saw them through the binoculars, they were glowing,' she said, 'and I definitely saw fluttering wings.' But even as she said the words, she wondered if it had been a dream.

'You know, my grandma used to say that mushrooms have magical powers,' said Fujiko. 'In Japan, there's a mushroom called lingzhi which is supposed to make people live for ever. And there are the kodama – forest spirits.'

Shyla wondered if the lights she had seen through the binoculars could have been the spirits of the forest...

'Can you hear that? The *tik-tik-tik*?' asked Benji.

'It's a blackbird. But I haven't seen one in the woods for ages!'

Shyla took the binoculars carefully out of her pocket. She searched the trees but didn't see anything unusual.

But when she turned back to look at the mushrooms, she froze. The pixie ring was glowing and the air around it was filled with a magical flutter. Delicate creatures with pale blue wings danced and twirled through the air. She could see their faces, and one of them turned to look directly at her.

'I can see them,' Shyla whispered to the rest of the gang. 'So many fairies!'

# CHAPTER 3
## A SECRET MESSAGE

The Explorers passed the binoculars to each other. Shyla was so eager to look at the fairies again she had to lock her fingers together to stop herself from grabbing them.

'I don't see anything,' said Fujiko.

'Me neither,' said Trix.

'Maybe they only want Shyla to see them,' Benji suggested. 'Tell us, what are they like?'

'It's as if I'm seeing another world,' said Shyla breathlessly. 'They're tiny, but they move fast.'

Suddenly, the largest fairy with the sapphire blue wings noticed she was being watched. She looked straight at Shyla.

Shyla could see her mouth move, as if the fairy was trying to tell her something. One by one, all the fairies turned in her direction. Shyla felt sure they had been waiting for this moment for a very long time.

Then the blue fairy pointed, motioning for Shyla to follow.

The fairy flew upwards, then whizzed back, as if to check that her human friends were right behind. That's when Shyla realised there were more of them. Little lights gleamed from behind every mushroom, and the air was full of the fluttering of wings.

'Come on. They're taking us somewhere!' Shyla shouted to the rest of the gang. 'Follow me!'

They ran to the edge of Bluebell Clearing, through a cluster of willow trees, onto the path beside the Tadpole Run.

'What can you see, Shyla?' asked Benji, trying to keep up with her. 'Where is she taking us?'

'I don't know. But she's leading us somewhere!'

They stopped by the side of the Tadpole Run, breathing hard. Through the binoculars, Shyla saw the blue fairy spinning in the air.

Then, out of nowhere, there was an explosion of colour and the empty stream filled with life.

A family of frogs sat on the bank opposite, their throats moving with every *ribbit*. Under the clear water, where an old, orange plastic bag had floated, there was now a beautiful minnow, followed by three smaller fish. Dragonflies hovered over the stream, and Shyla spotted the furry snout of an otter peeking out from behind a log.

## SUPER WOODLAND FACT:
**Wildlife that lives in freshwater streams**

**Frogs** have special skin that keeps them wet and happy. That's why they love ponds and lakes.

**Water Striders** have long, thin legs that help them glide on the water's surface.

**Freshwater fish**: there are over 10,000 different species of freshwater fish in the world, including trout and minnows!

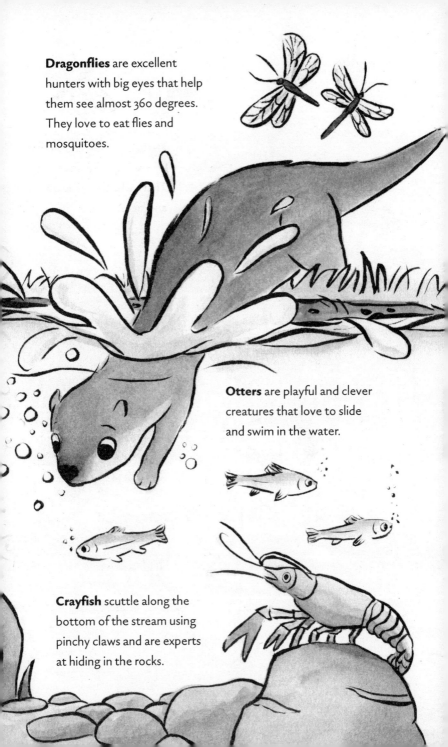

**Dragonflies** are excellent hunters with big eyes that help them see almost 360 degrees. They love to eat flies and mosquitoes.

**Otters** are playful and clever creatures that love to slide and swim in the water.

**Crayfish** scuttle along the bottom of the stream using pinchy claws and are experts at hiding in the rocks.

'Wow!' said Shyla. She passed the binoculars to Fujiko.

'I can see the animals!' gasped Fujiko, amazed. 'Everyone, come and look!'

Ajay went next, then Eric and Trix. Benji, who was last, took the longest time to look. 'I think the fairies want to show us what the stream could look like. But the trouble is we have no idea what to do!'

Shyla took the binoculars back. It seemed that only she could see the fairies. The blue fairy was now hovering above the water, in the same spot as a blue crisp packet. It was the exact colour of her dress.

Shyla tried to remember what Mr Mattison had taught them about streams. She knew that trees played an important role.

## SHYLA'S NOTEBOOK

**Trees near streams are like nature's superheroes! They do lots of cool things:**

🌿 **Stop flooding**: they help prevent water from overflowing the riverbank.

🌿 **Make homes for creatures**: animals love living in and around trees.

🌿 **Give shade**: they help keep the water the right temperature.

🌿 **Create safe spaces for fish**: fallen trees provide places for fish to hide and lay their eggs.

🌿 **Keep the water clean**: they stop bad chemicals from farms getting into the water.

But there were already a lot of trees around the stream – the only problem was their roots were home to old crisp packets, empty plastic bottles and dirty cans.

'It's the rubbish. We need to start with the rubbish!' Shyla realised.

'You mean we have to clear the stream?' asked Eric.

'Exactly.'

There was a rustling sound and an excited shout.

'Oh, there you are! Thank goodness!' said Mr Mattison, his face red. 'Leon told me you'd disappeared. You can't go running off like that!'

'I'm sorry,' Shyla stammered. 'I saw something from my bedroom window last night, and we wanted to investigate. It's my fault...'

'And then we saw the stream was so polluted,' said Trix. 'It's not right. We need to help!'

'I haven't been to this part of the wood in a while. It does look a lot worse than it used to,' Mr Mattison agreed. 'But I still expect you to follow my instructions. I'm disappointed in you.'

The gang went back to Swallow Clearing. Leon watched smugly as Mr Mattison told the class that nobody was allowed to stray out of view while they were in the woods. Fujiko's face burned with embarrassment.

The Woodland Explorers were careful to be

on their best behaviour for the rest of the day. At lunchtime, they came up with a plan.

'Let's do a Saturday Sweep!' said Trix excitedly, sandwich crumbs spilling from her mouth.

'What do you mean?'

## SHYLA'S NOTEBOOK
### Top ways to help the environment

1. **Pick up litter**: join a local clean-up crew to keep parks, streets and rivers free from litter.

2. **Plant a tree**: join a community tree-planting event to provide a home for wildlife.

3. **Reduce, reuse, recycle**: sort and recycle your waste. Find creative ways to reuse your rubbish!

4. **Save water**: turn off taps when not in use and fix leaks. Every drop counts!

5. **Start a garden**: grow your own fruits, vegetables or flowers to help the insects.

6. **Spread the word**: tell friends and family about the importance of caring for the environment. Inspire them to take action too!

'We'll spend a morning cleaning up as much of the woods as possible, particularly around the Tadpole Run.'

'You seriously want to spend your Saturday clearing rubbish?' asked Ajay. 'I'm going to the library to find out more about the history of Willow Wish Woods.'

'Couldn't you look it up on the internet?' asked Eric.

'There's not much online. In the library, I found a brilliant book about the woods.'

'But helping the woods will be like bringing history back to life,' Shyla pointed out.

'I'm not sure it's a good idea,' said Fujiko.

'Why?' asked Shyla, surprised. Fujiko usually loved helping the environment.

'You remember the Japanese legend of the kodama I told you about? I just realised how similar our fairies are...'

'Who are the kodama?' Benji asked, careful to keep his voice low so the rest of the lunchroom wouldn't hear. This was the Woodland Explorers' secret after all.

'Kodama are spirits that live in the heart of ancient trees. They've been around for centuries, watching over the forests. They protect the woods and everything that lives there. But they also give warnings. When you hear them rustling the leaves or making animal sounds, they're telling you that something bad might happen.'

'But the fairies wanted us to follow them,' said Shyla, confused. 'You saw the animals in the stream. The blue fairy wanted to show us what the stream could be like if we helped to look after it.'

'Or maybe she was telling us these animals have been chased away by something. Maybe something terrible...'

'Is this what happens in the story of the kodama?' asked Eric, his eyes wide.

'There are many kodama fairy tales. Sometimes they save people from monsters.'

'It didn't seem like something bad was about to happen, though,' said Ajay.

'But don't you see – it already did!' said Fujiko. 'We got into trouble with Mr Mattison. It was a sign we shouldn't have gone there.'

'That was Leon's fault, because he's a snitch!' said Trix.

'I don't want to do the Saturday Sweep,' said Fujiko. 'I'm scared something bad might happen.'

'OK,' said Shyla. Usually she would allow someone else to make decisions for her. But not this time. Shyla had never felt so strongly about anything before. 'That's fine, Fujiko. I'm still going to do it, though. Anyone else who would like to can come along. I'll be waiting for you in Bluebell Clearing at 11 a.m. tomorrow.'

# CHAPTER 4
## THE CLEAN-UP

Next morning, Shyla got up early. Excitement fizzed inside her. Even if none of the Woodland Explorers came, she knew she'd be doing something good for the fairies and the forest.

As they were packing raisin pancakes, cheese bites and other picnic snacks into a bag, Shyla asked her mum:

'Did Nani ever say anything unusual about her binoculars?'

'She said they gave her a better view of the world,' said Mum, looking at Shyla carefully. 'And they helped her learn about things that others couldn't always see. I never really understood what she meant... Why do you ask?'

'I just wondered, that's all,' said Shyla quickly.

She had Nani's binoculars tucked into the pocket of her dungarees. She'd decided not to show their special power to any of the adults. That would be the Woodland Explorers' secret.

Benji and Eric were waiting for her at the end of the path with Benji's dog, Nelson. He was sniffing something in the nearby bushes and his tail wagged excitedly.

'We're with you for the sweep,' said Eric. 'We want to help.' Then they bumped into Ajay and Aunty Kali leaving their house with a wheelbarrow.

'It's to move the rubbish,' Ajay announced.

'Brilliant!' said Shyla. It would be much easier with their help.

'Why is Fujiko scared of the fairies?' Ajay asked, as they took turns pushing the wheelbarrow down Woodland Walk. 'There's nothing to be afraid of.'

'Try to put yourself in her shoes. Sometimes the unknown is scary. But *you're* never scared of anything,' said Shyla.

'Only spiders. Big, hairy ones,' Ajay admitted.

'And Trix is scared of worms. They make her go all squirmy,' Benji said.

'Do you think Trix will come?' asked Shyla.

'Yeah, I'm sure she will,' said Benji. 'You know Trix! Anything for an adventure.'

He was right. As they approached Bluebell Clearing, Shyla saw her with her dad and brothers.

The sun was out, bouncing off puddles that hadn't fully dried up. Trix's little brothers jumped in them, spraying muddy water in all directions. Nobody minded – the Explorers were on a mission, but it could still be fun.

Shyla's mum, Aunty Kali and Trix's dad arranged their lunch on a big tree stump as the gang worked.

There was more to do than they'd thought. Ajay and Shyla stepped into the stream in their wellies. They put on the colourful rubber gloves that they'd brought with them and carefully plucked out plastic bags, cans and chocolate wrappers, which they put in huge bin bags.

'Hey, look, it's a zombie,' said Ajay, holding up an old doll. Its face was smeared with dirt, and one of its legs was missing. Nelson sniffed it, then carried it in his mouth to the rubbish pile.

'Good dog,' said Trix, patting him on the head.

They found fishing tackle, rusted bicycle parts and a tyre, half-buried in the mud.

Eric and Benji picked up all the food wrappers, plastic bottles, tissues and other rubbish they found among the trees. Trix carefully emptied all the bags and sorted the rubbish into four bigger sacks, so that some things could be recycled.

'This stuff has been here a long time,' said Ajay. 'The sell-by date on this crisp packet is from two years ago!'

'I know. Plastic takes ages to decompose,' Shyla said. She remembered Mum telling her about this when they were on the beach last year, picking rubbish as they walked.

'What does that mean? Decompose?' asked Eric.

'It's nature's way of recycling. When something decomposes, it turns into smaller pieces. Then it goes back into the earth to become part of the soil again.'

'How long does it take?'

'Plastic can take hundreds of years!'

# SHYLA'S NOTEBOOK
How long does rubbish take to decompose?

**Banana peel**: up to 2 years

**Newspaper**: 2-6 weeks

**Apple core**: 2 months

**Cardboard**: 2 months to 3 years

**Cotton T-shirt**: up to 6 months

**Plastic bottle**: 450 years or more

**Aluminium can**: 200-500 years

**Glass bottle**: over 1 million years

'So this plastic bottle could still be here when our great-great-great-grandchildren are alive?'

'Yep! But we're taking it to be recycled, so it won't be!' Shyla said happily.

In the end, it took three trips to the recycling

bank before the gang managed to clear all the rubbish.

'Hey, look,' said Shyla. 'This bottle is the same shade as the blue fairy's wings. I wonder what her name could be?'

That's when she realised she already knew. *Sapphira*. It was the name Shyla had secretly given her when she first saw her.

'It's beautiful,' said Trix.

As everyone tucked into lunch, Shyla sneaked away to peer through her binoculars. She looked around for Sapphira, but couldn't see her. The world she saw through the lens was the same as the one everyone else could see.

Her heart sank. They hadn't done enough.

'What's wrong?' asked Trix, who had come to find her.

'I can't see any fairies or animals,' said Shyla, blinking away tears. She had been so certain their plan would work.

'Maybe that's not what Sapphira meant,' suggested Trix. 'Maybe she was trying to tell us something else.'

'Or maybe Fujiko was right,' said Shyla quietly.

# CHAPTER 5
## FROGS FIRST

That night, Ajay came round to Shyla's for a sleepover. Shyla's mum made her favourite tortilla wraps for dinner, but Shyla still hadn't cheered up. Ajay seemed excitable. It was as if he didn't care that the gang's plan hadn't worked. Shyla wished he would go home so she could be alone.

'Want to go to your shed?' he asked.

'It's not a shed – it's an art studio,' she said crossly. 'We can if you want.'

They walked down the garden towards the brightly-coloured studio. Shyla and her mum had spent the summer painting it. There were pictures of every bird they'd met in the forest. Ajay stopped to admire a new one – a robin Shyla had seen on

her garden fence last week and had had to paint right away.

'He's great,' he said. 'From a distance he looks real.'

'Thanks. Anyway, how come you're so happy?'

'I found something in the library this afternoon,' Ajay said. 'It's the first of three books – on the history of Willow Wish Woods.'

'Oh, yes. I remember you mentioned that book,' Shyla said, moving pots of paintbrushes out of the way so they could sit down. 'But aren't you worried about the *future* of the woods? Lots of animals have already gone. What if the ones that are left disappear too?'

She thought of the birds painted on her shed – the red-breasted robin, the striped woodpecker, the flashy jay, and the beautiful chaffinch with its pink, blue and black feathers. What if they no longer wanted to live here either? What if there really was danger lurking – something that was scaring them away?

It made her think she should say sorry to Fujiko for not listening to her. Shyla felt bad that her friend had missed out on spending Saturday with the rest of the gang.

'This afternoon, at the end of the picnic, I had a look through your binoculars,' said Ajay. 'Sorry; I shouldn't have taken them without asking, but I put them straight back.'

'It doesn't matter,' Shyla sighed. 'The fairies were gone. There was nobody there.'

'What if I told you...' said Ajay, raising his eyebrows '... that I saw something?'

'What?'

'It was a bright blue light dancing in the roots of the willow tree. Right next to a frog!'

'You think it could have been Sapphira?'

Ajay nodded.

'You're not just saying this to make me feel better?'

'I never lie,' said Ajay, looking hurt.

'So you can see her too! But where did the rest of the frogs go?'

'I don't know for sure, but I have an idea.'

'Go on...'

'Well, the Willow Wish Woods history book I found in the library is super long. I haven't had time to finish the first chapter yet. But I read something important. It said that willow trees have grown in the woods for hundreds of years. And the Tadpole Run has always been a home for frogs!'

'Wow... but what does that mean?' asked Shyla.

'I don't know...' said Ajay.

That's when they heard footsteps coming down the garden path.

'It's probably Mum bringing snacks!'

Then the handle turned, and Eric's face appeared round the door.

'I heard you from my garden. Dad said I could see you before bed.'

They quickly filled him in on what Ajay had seen. Eric's eyes widened. He rapped his fingers on the side of the table, which he always did when he was thinking.

'You know when Mr Mattison was telling us about mushrooms and the Wood Wide Web?'

'Yes,' said Shyla.

'You first saw the fairies by the mushrooms... Do you think they're part of the Wood Wide Web too? Maybe the fairies help spread information around the woods?'

'Yes!' said Ajay, jumping up. 'Maybe that's what they're up to – telling the frogs what we're doing. Then they'll spread the word to other creatures.'

'You think so?' asked Shyla, happiness swelling in her chest. 'So, what can we do?'

'We need to learn more about frogs,' said Ajay. 'What habitat they like to live in. What they need to survive.'

'We've cleared the stream already,' said Eric. 'But we can do more. Mr Mattison told us they lay eggs when spring comes. Hopefully we'll get tadpoles. It's called the Tadpole Run for a reason, right?'

'Exactly – and we'll help it live up to its name!' Shyla decided.

# CHAPTER 6
## A BIGGER MISSION

At break time on Monday, the Woodland Explorers gathered in a corner of the playground. They needed to discuss everything they'd found out.

But Fujiko didn't join them. Instead, she pulled a book out of her bag and pretended to read. Shyla noticed she kept looking over in their direction.

Shyla felt cross. Couldn't Fujiko see they wanted to do something good? Didn't she want to be a Woodland Explorer?

She was about to say something when she noticed how upset Fujiko was. Behind her book, her friend's shoulders were hunched. She looked like she might cry.

Shyla went over to Fujiko and put her arms around her.

'Hi, Fujiko,' she said. 'Why are you sad?'

Fujiko covered her eyes to stop the tears, but she didn't say anything.

Then Shyla heard her whisper: 'I'm scared.'

'Of what?'

'I'm scared of doing the wrong thing. Maybe the kodama are warning us? That's why we got into trouble with Mr Mattison. But if we don't do anything, more and more animals will disappear from the woods.'

Shyla realised then how similar she and Fujiko were.

'I know,' she said. 'I'm confused too. But clearing rubbish from the stream feels like the right thing to do.'

'Why?'

'Do you remember when Mr Mattison was telling us about habitats? That they need to provide everything for animals to survive, like

food, water and shelter? It's like us in our homes. We want our houses to be comfy and safe. But with all this litter around, the habitats are being destroyed. So we need to do everything we can to clean them up. I think that's what Sapphira, the blue fairy, is trying to tell us.'

Fujiko nodded slowly. 'I don't think the kodama can be angry if they know we're trying to help,' she said quietly.

Then a thought came to Shyla.

'Do you think their warning is not about a monster, but about us humans? About what will happen if we keep treating the woods badly?'

'Wow. Maybe,' said Fujiko, putting her book down. 'You could be right.'

Shyla pulled her friend to her feet and together they joined the rest of the gang.

'I know all about tadpoles,' Trix was saying. 'My grandma used to have some in her pond. They need a nice, sunny spot and lots of fresh water.'

# SUPER WOODLAND FACT:
## What tadpoles need to survive

**Clean water:** tadpoles need clean,
fresh water that is free of pollution.

**Safe shelter:** tadpoles need safe places to rest.
They like to hide in shallow areas, among rocks or plants.

**Food:** at first, tadpoles eat only a little food. But as they grow,
tadpoles develop big appetites! They eat algae, plants and tiny
organisms found in the water.

**Sunlight:** tadpoles need light, but not too much.
Trees and leaves provide the shade they need to grow.

**Oxygen:** just like us, tadpoles need oxygen to breathe.
They get oxygen from the water through their gills.

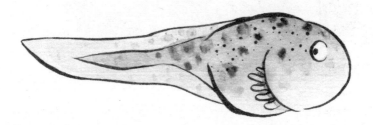

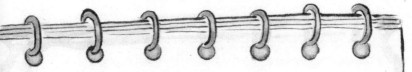

# SHYLA'S NOTEBOOK

## How tadpoles turn into frogs

**Tadpole beginnings:** tadpoles start as tiny eggs laid in the water and once they've hatched, swim using their tails.

**Growing-up tadpole:** tadpoles breathe through gills, eating algae and plants, and as they grow, develop back legs first, then front legs.

**Tail transformation:** when tadpoles lose their tails, they change into frogs and can breathe air.

**Hopping into frog life:** frogs explore both land and water, using their powerful legs for jumping and catching insects with their long, sticky tongues.

'Do you think the water in the Tadpole Run is fresh?' asked Ajay.

'It's probably better now that we've cleaned up the rubbish. But people keep littering, don't they?' said Trix crossly. 'They might drop plastic bottles, wrappers and packets further upstream and then the rubbish floats all the way down. The water will keep being polluted.'

'We could do a Saturday Sweep every week?' suggested Benji.

'No, that doesn't make sense,' said Shyla. 'We need to stop people from throwing rubbish in the first place.'

'But how?'

'Maybe we should put up signs,' suggested Fujiko shyly. 'They wouldn't just say "Stop Littering". They'd show pictures of all the animals and plants harmed by the litter.'

'Yes, that's an amazing idea!' said Benji, clapping his hands. 'Shyla, I think we need another club badge. Should it be a fairy?'

'Oh, yes!' said Shyla. 'But a mushroom, not a fairy. Mushrooms are where all of this began.'

'Perfect!'

'I'll work on them tonight. But what about the signs?'

'We'll need to ask Mr Mattison whether we can put them up around the woods. Do you think he'll say yes?' asked Fujiko.

'There's only one way to find out!' said Trix.

Shyla decided to ask right after break. Mr Mattison thought it was a great idea. He said he'd speak to Mrs Jay, the headteacher, and she might have to contact the Woodland Trust. But he thought they could put signs up around school.

'We can get started in our art lesson today,' he promised, and then he invited Shyla to tell the rest of the class about her idea.

Shyla normally didn't like talking in front of

big groups, but this time was different. It might be the Woodland Explorers' only chance to bring the creatures back.

After lunch, Shyla began the art lesson by saying:

'I want your help with a special mission. Some of you might have noticed the rubbish in our woods. It's particularly bad around the Tadpole Run and Bluebell Clearing. We think it's the reason why so many animals who used to live here don't want to any more. We owe it to them to protect the woodland. Maybe if we do, they'll come back to their habitats.'

Leon and Cora whispered loudly about how the gang only discovered the rubbish because they ran away in the lesson. But the rest of Pine Class listened and wanted to help.

Everyone got into pairs, and Mr Mattison handed out big sheets of card. Shyla worked with Trix on a frog-shaped sign which she hoped would one day go next to the stream.

Later, when everyone hung up their signs to dry, Shyla was amazed at how good they were.

Shyla and Ajay were chatting about their plan as they walked home with Aunty Kali, when Ajay had an idea.

'Mum, can we stop off at Bluebell Clearing? Just for half an hour before dinner?' he asked.

Aunty Kali agreed and talked on the phone to Shyla and Ajay's grandpa as they searched for rocks and stones around the stream.

'Trix was saying that a safe shelter is important for tadpoles,' said Ajay. 'And this is the willow tree where I last saw Sapphira. Let's build some natural shelters on the banks of the stream to help the tadpoles. Then Sapphira might appear.'

'Look, there are some mossy rocks, next to the pine trees!' cried Shyla.

They carried the best ones to the edge of the riverbank. Some were bulky and heavy. They were careful not to drop them on their feet.

Ajay wedged the bigger ones among the roots of the willow tree. Then they put the heaviest one on the other side of the riverbank. It jutted out into the middle of the water like a rocky pier.

When they had finished Ajay sat down on a tree stump to rest.

'Shall we have a look through the binoculars?' he whispered, glancing at his mum to check she was still speaking on the phone.

Shyla pulled them from her bag. She felt nervous as she looked through the lens.

But before she had scanned both banks of

the stream, she sensed there was nothing there.

Ajay spent ages looking through the binoculars, peering under every root and rock. Then he shook his head.

He squeezed Shyla's hand. 'We'll keep trying,' he said, but she could hear the disappointment in his voice.

*Hoo hoo. Hoo hoo.*

Shyla had just fallen asleep. She'd spent the evening working on the mushroom badges, though her heart had not been in it.

The owl hoot woke her up. At first, Shyla pulled the duvet over her head, but then it sounded again.

She ran to the window and gasped. In Bluebell Clearing, the pixie ring was glowing bright.

Shyla picked up Nani's binoculars from the windowsill, opened the window, and dared to look out. It took a few seconds for her eyes to take in the shimmer of fairies sitting on the mushrooms. She followed the ring with her binoculars and saw a tiny creature on every one. They were all facing in one direction, as if waiting for something.

Shyla held her breath. Then, suddenly, she was there. Sapphira appeared from a gap in the roots below the willow tree, where Ajay had arranged mossy rocks a few hours before.

With shimmering wings, she danced through the air. At first, she was just a flash of light. But as Shyla watched, the fairy grew bigger and bigger, drawing closer to her window.

Then Sapphira was hovering right in front of her, and Shyla felt a spark of connection.

'I thought that you'd gone,' she whispered.

Sapphira shook her head. Her eyes were full of the wisdom of ancient forests.

'We're clearing the woods for the animals. We're telling everyone to keep the Tadpole Run clean. The Woodland Explorers promise we'll do all we can to make this a safe place for creatures to live. Will you... will you help spread the word about our work?'

The blue fairy flew closer still, as if to show she was truly listening. She was so close now that Shyla could make out her golden freckles and long eyelashes curling up to her fringe. She nodded quickly and beamed. Before Shyla could say anything else, she darted off into the moonlight.

As they put up signs around school the next day, Shyla told the Woodland Explorers about her midnight meeting with Sapphira. It seemed no one else had seen the glowing light from Bluebell Clearing.

'It wasn't your owl hoot?' Shyla asked Benji.

'Not this time. It must have been a real owl.'

'I wonder what she was trying to tell you. It must mean our plan to save the animals is working,' said Trix.

Shyla handed out the mushroom badges that she had made the night before.

'These are great,' said Benji. 'They'll remind us of our mission!'

'So what should we do next?' asked Shyla.

'We could do more research into animal habitats,' said Ajay, fiddling with his pin. 'I've found a good website on my tablet.'

'Or we can see whether the Emerald King has any clues,' said Benji. 'After all, our club started with him.'

'Great idea!' Shyla said. She loved the old oak tree. He was filled with magic and wisdom – just like Sapphira. If only she could work out what the fairy wanted to tell her.

'Here's to solving our mission!' said Trix, and the Woodland Explorers put their hands together.

'*Hoo-hoo, hoo-hoo.*' The sound of their owl hoot echoed through the forest.

In Swallow Clearing, Mr Mattison was teaching Pine Class about the creatures that liked to eat mushrooms and the role they play in the forest ecosystem. He had written interesting facts on cards which he hung from the Learning Tree.

RABBITS LOVE DIGGING UP MUSHROOMS WHICH HELPS TO SPREAD SEEDS, ENCOURAGING PLANTS TO GROW.

DEER CAN SAFELY EAT MANY MUSHROOMS THAT WOULD BE POISONOUS TO HUMANS.

WILD BOAR HAVE A GOOD SENSE OF SMELL, MAKING THEM SKILLED TRUFFLE HUNTERS, DIGGING BELOW THE SURFACE.

SQUIRRELS MAINLY FEAST ON NUTS, ACORNS AND FRUIT. THEY ALSO HAVE A TASTE FOR TRUFFLE—LIKE MUSHROOMS. THEY DIG THEM UP AND LEAVE THEM TO DRY ON BRANCHES BEFORE ENJOYING THEIR MEAL.

It made Shyla think of Braveheart, the stag they had rescued last spring after his antler got tangled in a net. They had planned a rescue operation for him with help from the Emerald King. Shyla realised how much she missed the ruler of the trees.

'Benji's right. Let's go and see the king,' she whispered to Trix. They were sitting on their colourful cushions around the Learning Tree, working on the next stage of their mushroom projects. Mr Mattison had asked them to make a poster showing why mushrooms were important to forest life.

Trix nodded and passed the message to Ajay, who whispered it to the rest of the gang. Quietly, they headed to their special meeting spot through the gap between the pines. Shyla was amazed by the way the Emerald King's song could be heard as soon as they stepped into the clearing. It always gave away his mood. Today a lively tune filled the air. Shyla felt a seed of hope sprout inside of her.

'Sorry we've been away so long,' said Benji, walking over to touch the king's trunk. 'We didn't forget about you—'

'Something looks different,' said Eric, interrupting him.

'What do you mean?' asked Trix, looking around. 'It's the same old king. But it's autumn now and the leaves are changing.'

'It's more than that,' Eric said. 'Don't move. Listen.'

So each of the Woodland Explorers stood in silence, trying to pick up on any unusual sounds.

Then Shyla heard it. *Ribbit*.

'Frogs,' she whispered.

And there they were – two frogs sitting on the bank of the Tadpole Run.

'No way!' said Ajay.

'They've come back!' said Fujiko.

'This is incredible,' whispered Shyla.

Eric moved nearer the stream to take a better look. He turned around to the rest of the Woodland Explorers, smiling.

'They'll spread the word that the forest is safe to live in again,' he said excitedly. 'The frogs will let the other frogs know. They'll pass the message on to different creatures. And the trees will communicate through their underground root network, the Wood Wide Web!'

Shyla imagined all the mushrooms and the tree roots below ground, sending messages to each other. She felt for Nani's binoculars in her pocket and brought them to her eyes. When she looked through the lens at the Tadpole Run, she gasped.

She could see the frogs through her binoculars, but also many other creatures. Squirrels scurried along tree branches, their fluffy tails swaying like flags. Robins hopped along the ground, their red chests puffed out proudly. The head of a rabbit poked up from between some bushes. Colourful birds flitted among the treetops, their voices blending with the song of the Emerald King.

And then she spotted him in the middle of the clearing – Braveheart, the stag they had rescued.

'You came back,' said Shyla, amazed. But Braveheart was there in real life, not just in Nani's binoculars. And she could see Sapphira on top of the stag's head. The fairy waved at Shyla and gave her the most brilliant smile.

'I can see her!' shouted Eric. 'I can see Sapphira!'

'I can too,' said Benji in awe. 'I can see all of them!'

'Woah!' cried Trix. 'Do you think they came back because of us?'

Shyla felt as though she was being lifted up on an invisible string.

'I think they have,' she said. 'There's so much left to do. But we've made a start!'

'We'll keep going!' shouted Ajay, and Benji did his best ever owl hoot.

Then all the Woodland Explorers put their hands together and cheered.

That evening, Shyla sat in her art studio with her birthday inks and the wooden frame from the Woodland Explorers. She'd been longing to paint the kingfisher, but his picture would have to wait. There was someone else she knew the dazzling blue ink would be perfect for. She dipped her brush in the pot and began the outline of delicate fairy wings.

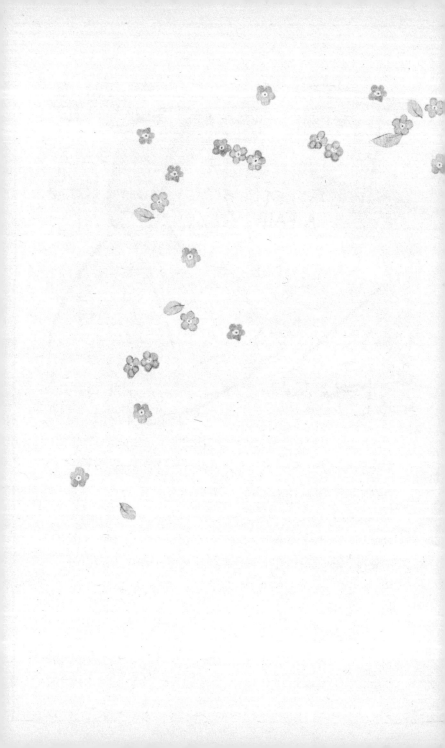

# LET'S BUILD
# A FAIRY GARDEN

Welcome to your magical
fairy garden adventure.

Follow these instructions to
create an enchanting world
for your little winged friends.

## 1. Choose the perfect spot:

Find a cosy corner in your garden . . .

...or a sunny windowsill where your fairies will be happy.

## 2. Gather your materials:

You'll need a big shallow container or pot to plant your seeds in. Some potting soil, moss and a packet of seeds.

Tiny flowers, such as forget-me-nots, pansies, or violas, are perfect for miniature gardens. These can be found in most garden centres.

You can also use stones and pebbles, fir cones, bark, shells and tree stumps.

### 3. Design your fairy garden:

Let your imagination run wild! Arrange the plants, rocks, and decorations to create a magical land. Create pathways with pebbles, build tiny houses using seashells and sticks, and design outdoor areas where your fairies can meet.

## 4. Create a pixie ring:
To make a pixie ring, gather a few small stones and arrange them in a circle on the soil – you can pretend they're tiny mushrooms. Legend has it that fairies dance in these rings under the light of the moon!

## 5. Care for your fairy garden:
Place your fairy garden in a sunny spot and water it regularly to keep the plants healthy.

## 6. Invite the fairies:

Once your magical garden is complete, invite the fairies to come and play! Leave a note or a small gift for them to find, and look out for signs of fairy dust!

## Join the Woodland Explorers Club

Discover the magic and mystery
of Willow Wish Woods.

Full of nature facts, animal
adventures, and forest school fun!

# JOIN THE WOODLAND EXPLORERS FOR MORE ADVENTURES.

## BENJI'S EMERALD KING

Willow Wish Woods is an ancient place of earth, leaves... and magic. But something is wrong and only Benji and his friends can bring the forest and its creatures back to life.

# AJAY AND THE RED-WINGED PRINCE

A story from the past about a kindly
prince inspires Ajay to stand up for
the plight of the red-winged thrush.

**Coming May 2025!**

# JOIN THE WOODLAND EXPLORERS FOR MORE ADVENTURES.